DOWN BY THE COOL OF THE POOL

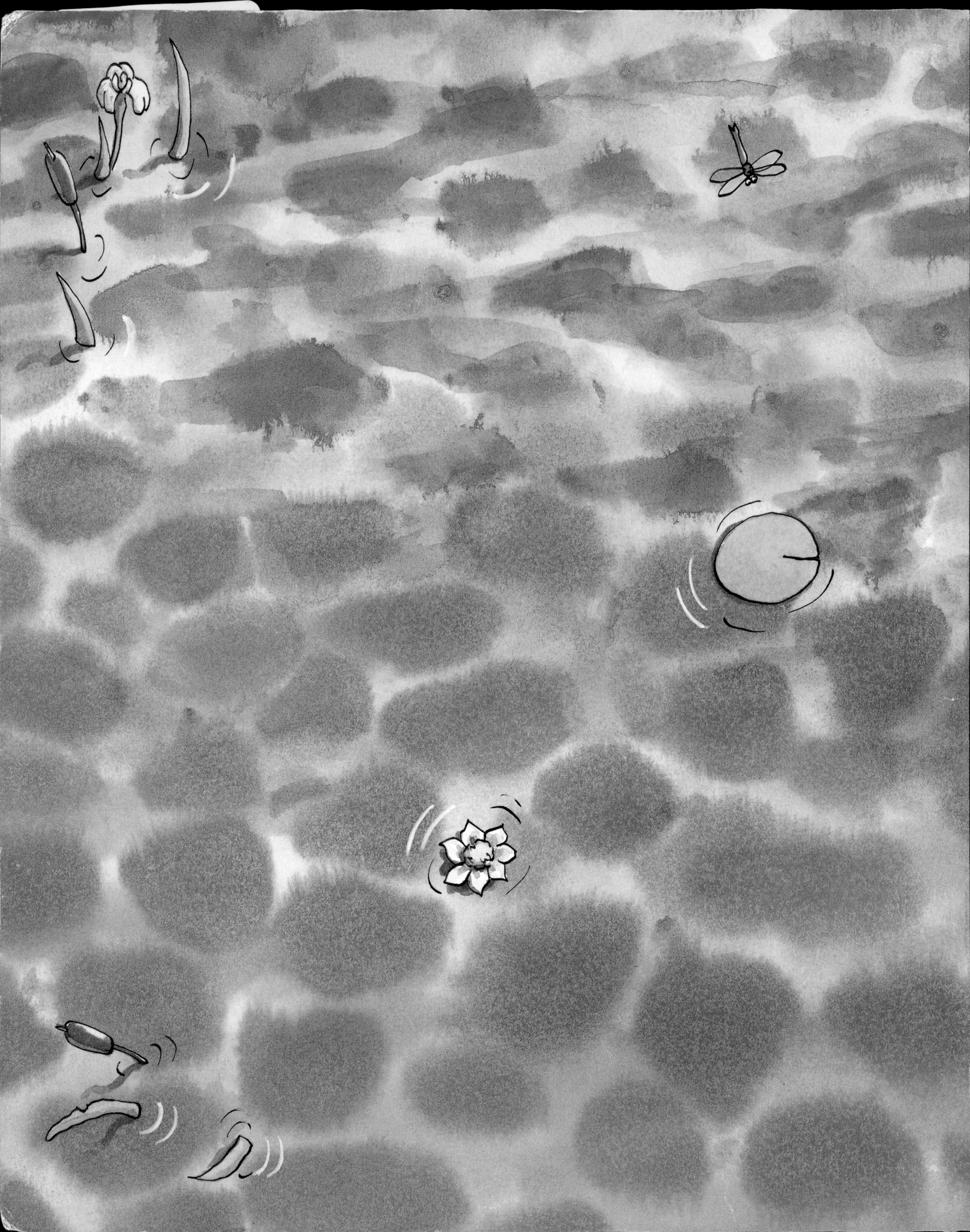

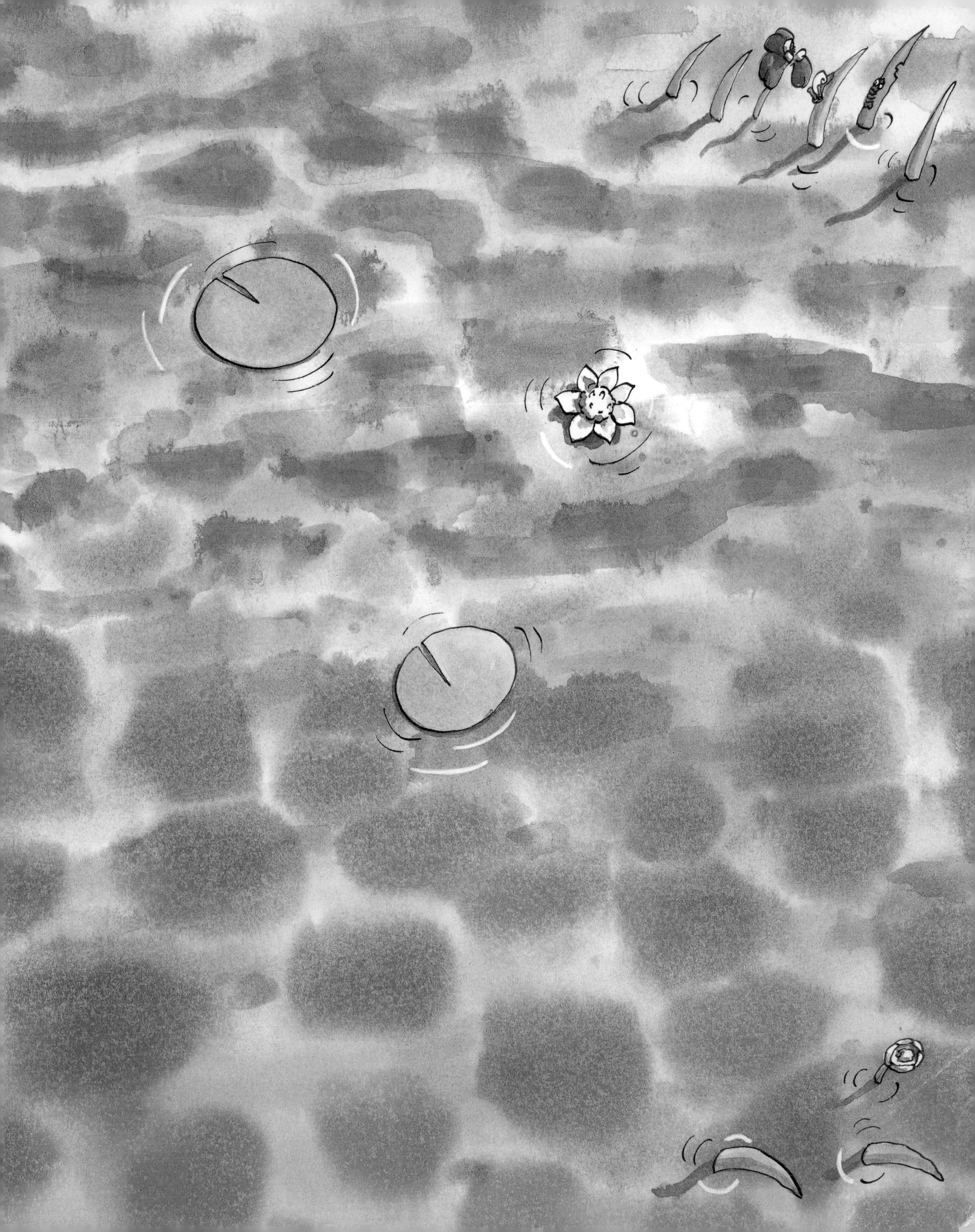

For George, Harriet, Doris and Guthrie,
and the cool of the pool in France – T.M.

For the lovely chucklesome little Joe – G.P-R.

ORCHARD BOOKS
338 Euston Road, London NW1 3BH
Orchard Books Australia
Level 17/207 Kent Street, Sydney, NSW 2000

ISBN 978 1 84121 098 8
First published in 2001 by Orchard Books
First published in paperback in 2002

A CIP catalogue record for this book is available from the British Library.

8 10 9
Printed in China

Orchard Books is a division of Hachette Children's Books
an Hachette UK company.
www.hachette.co.uk

DOWN BY THE COOL OF THE POOL
Tony Mitton
illustrated by Guy Parker-Rees
ORCHARD

Down by the pool
in the cool of the day,
Frog cried, "Wheeeee!
Can you dance like me?"

Duck came to see.
"I can dance too.
But not like you.
I can flap."

So Duck went "flap"

and Frog cried,

"Wheeeeee!

Can you dance like me?"

Down by the cool of the pool.

Pig came to see.
"I can dance too. But not like you.
I can wiggle."
So Pig went "wiggle",
Duck went "flap",

and Frog cried,
"Wheeeee!
Can you dance like me?"
Down by the cool of the pool.

Sheep came to see.
"I can dance too.
But not like you.
I can stamp."
So Sheep went
stamp,

Pig went "wiggle",

Duck went "flap",

and Frog cried "Wheeeee!

Can you dance like me?"

Down by the cool of the pool.

Then up sprang Cat
with a sudden bound
and Dog
came frisking
round and round.

Goat butted in
with a **skip**
and a **hop**,

and Frog cried,
"Wheeeee!
That's great! Don't stop."

Then Playful Pony
began to prance
and Donkey drummed his hoofbeat dance,

but when it came to Capering Cow,
Frog cried, "Wow! Altogether now..."

With a stamp and a wiggle,

and a "flap" and a
wheeeee!
the animals danced so joyfully,

till . . .
with a bump and a slip . . .
and a trip and a crash

and a "Whoops!
Watch out . . . !"
and a "topple", and a . . .

Splash!
into the pool they "flapped"
and they "flopped".

But did that stop them?

No! No! No!
For they all cried, "Ooh!" and,
"Whoooop!"
and "Wheeeee!"
"Come and see.
Oh, ha-ha-hee!

We're having fun, dancing our dance

in the cool of the pool!"

And they splished and splashed
till their dance was done,

then away they drifted

and down went the sun,

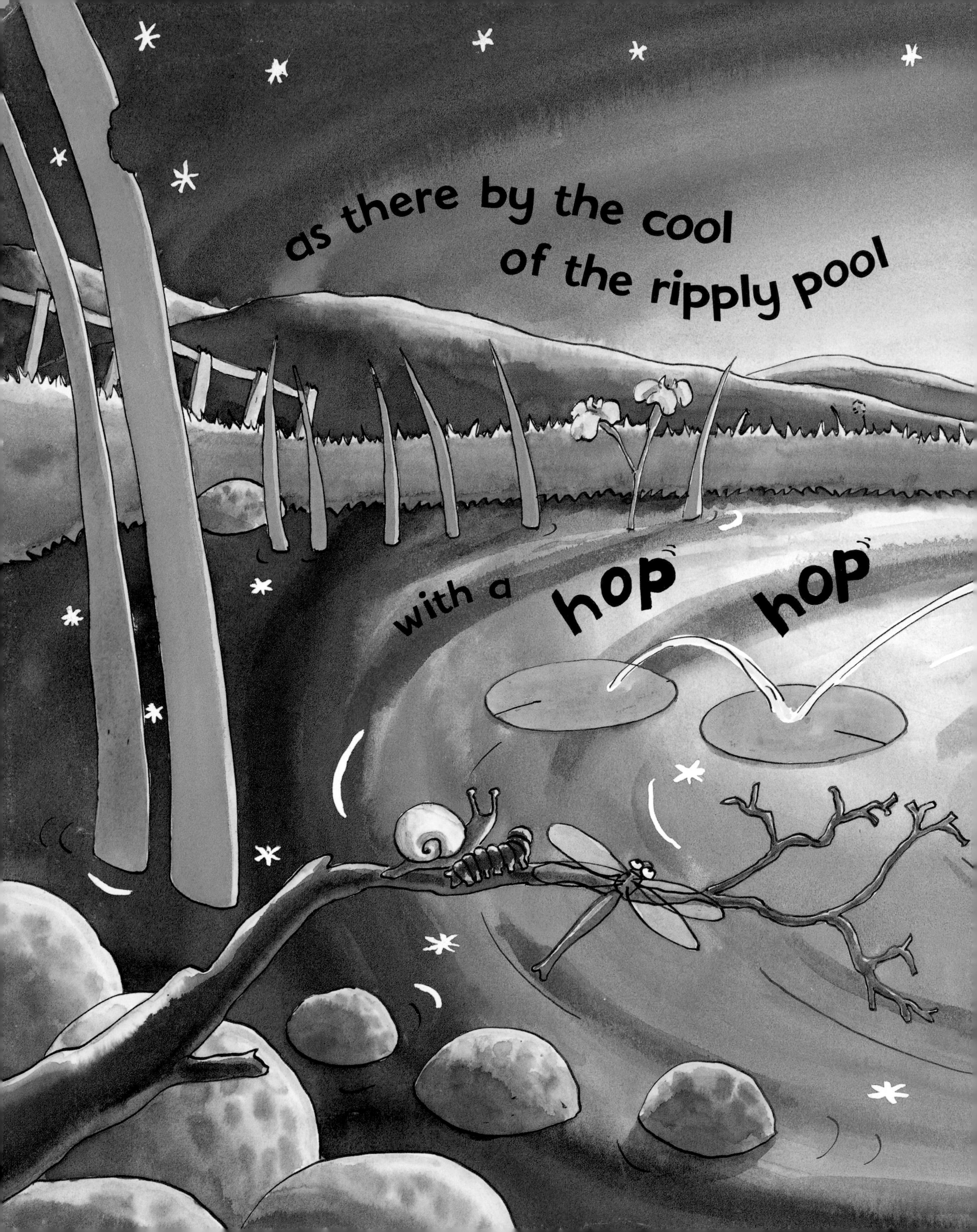
as there by the cool
of the ripply pool
with a hop hop

PLOP!
even Frog . . .
was gone.

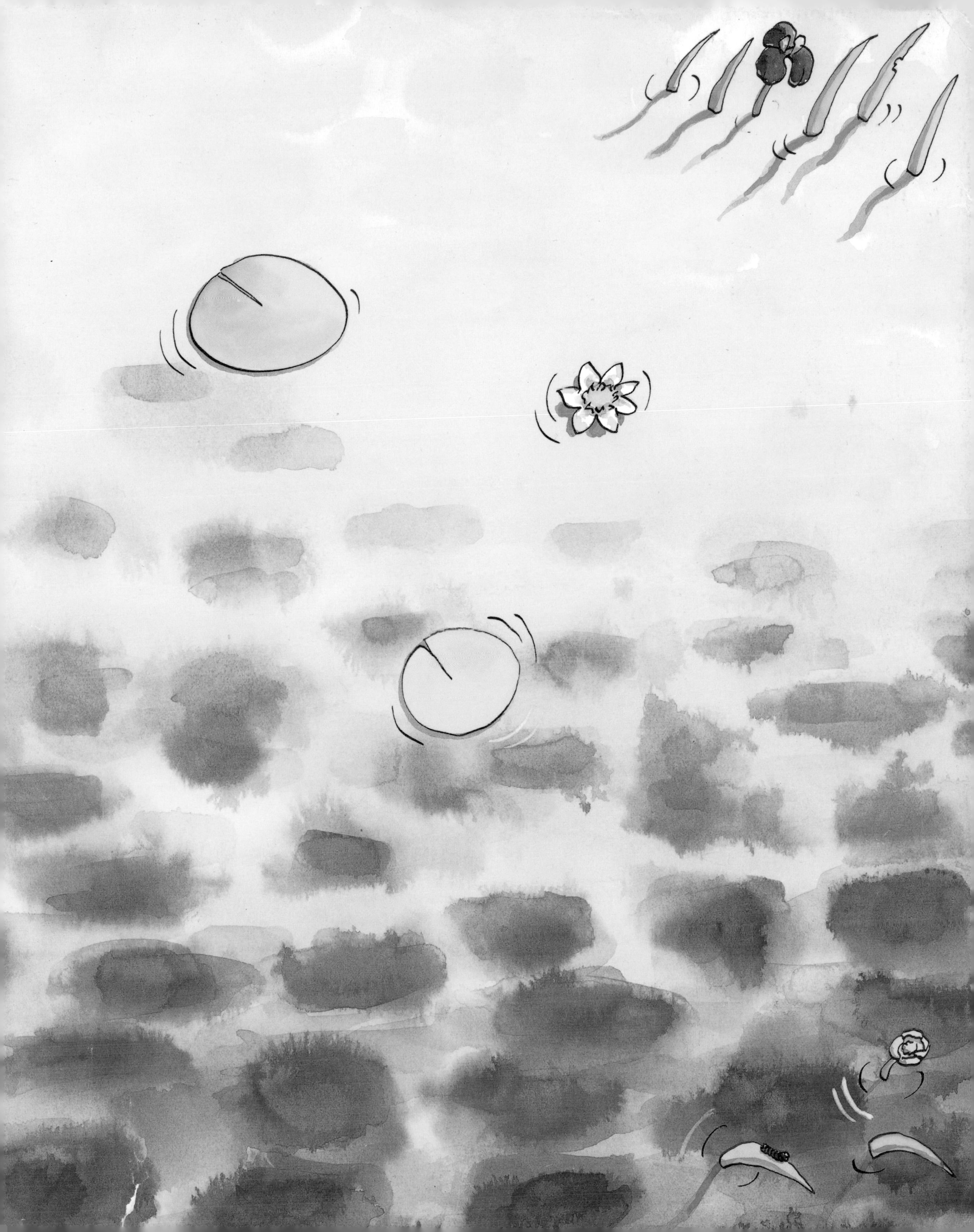